MY TRIP TO THE SCIENCE MUSEUM

BY MERCER MAYER

Dedicated to Dr. Neil deGrasse Tyson. Thanks for making the universe so much fun!

HARPER FESTIVAL
An Imprint of HarperCollins*Publishers*

HarperCollins Publishers 200 Since 1817

www.harpercollinschildrens.com
Library of Congress Control Number: 2015947483
ISBN 978-0-06-147809-3
17 18 19 20 21 CWM 10 9 8 7 6 5 4 3

A Big Tuna Trading Company, LLC/J. R. Sansevere Book
www.littlecritter.com
First Edition

It was Science Day and my class
took a bus to the science museum.

BUS 5

We met the museum's director.
His name was Dr. DaBison. He was
going to show us around.

He gave us special tags with our names on them.

There were all sorts of experiments that we could touch.
I played with a tornado machine.

They had a magnet so strong it lifted Gator off the floor. There was a giant magnifying glass that made Malcolm look so funny.

Dr. DaBison showed us how to make a battery out of a potato. Everyone got a potato, a light bulb, and some wires. Everyone made it work except me.

I wasn't really upset.

Miss Kitty and Dr. DaBison touched a plasma globe.
Their fur stuck out. They looked so silly.

Dr. DaBison showed us a wind tunnel. Then he and Miss Kitty jumped in and floated in the air, just like astronauts do in space.

Everyone wanted to do that. We yelled, "Me next! Me next!" but Miss Kitty said that we weren't big enough yet.

There were model Mars Rovers.
It was fun to race them.
Miss Kitty won!

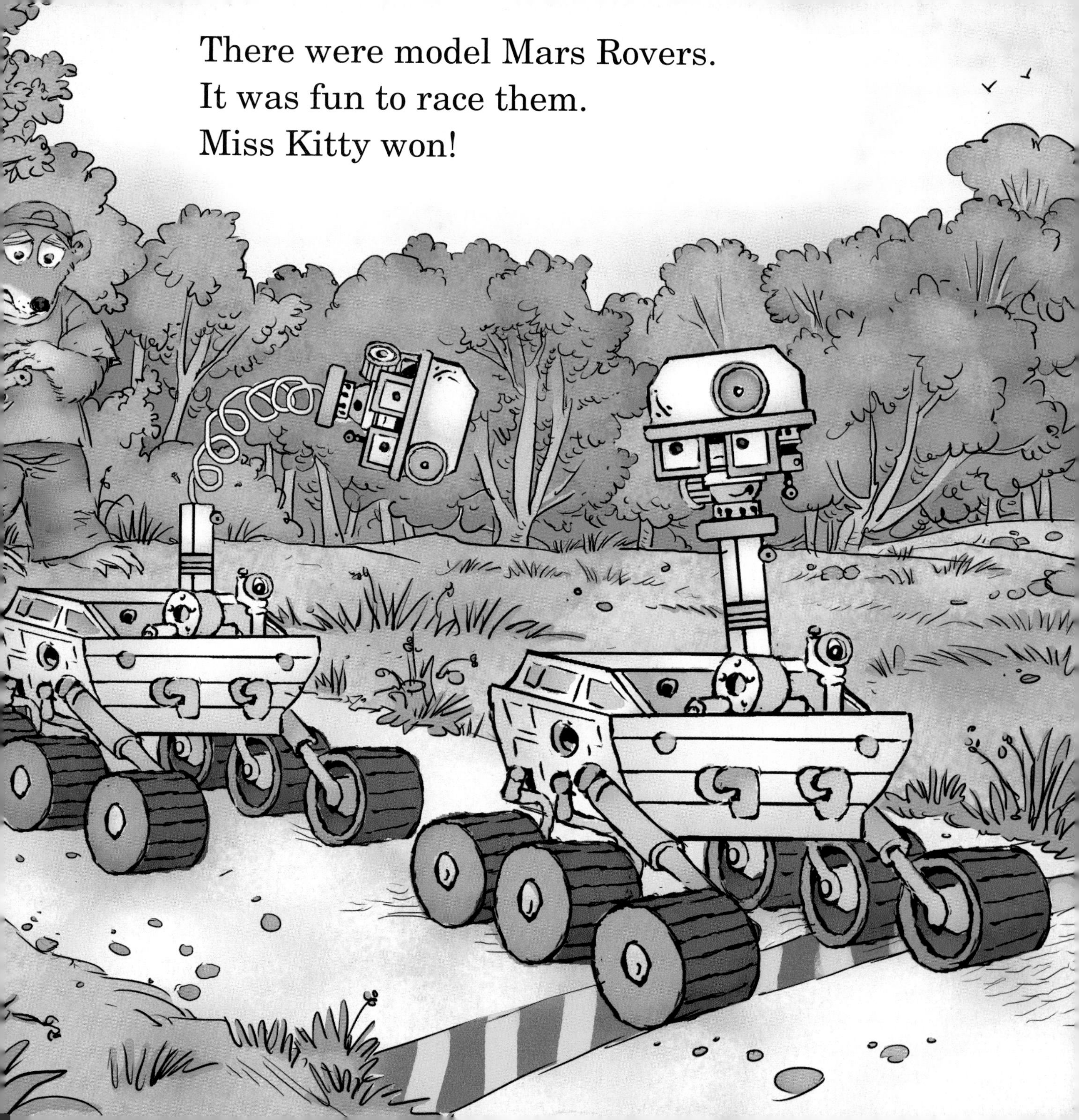

It was lunchtime. We got our lunches from our backpacks.
We had lunch outside on a big model of the space shuttle.

We even went inside. That was neat-o-rrific.

Dr. DaBison said it was time to go into the planetarium for a surprise. We all sat down and saw a big dome over our heads.

Then the lights went out. Dr. DaBison said,
"Get ready to fly through the universe."

Out of the darkness, the Earth came by us.
It was big. It was humongous!

We went farther. We saw planets and comets up close, like we were really there.

Then we flew deep into the universe . . .

. . billions of miles away. We were amazed! But not everyone.

The lights came back on. It was time to go.
Before we got on the bus, Miss Kitty said,
"What do we say to Dr. DaBison?"

We all said, “Thank you.”
Dr. DaBison asked, “What do you want to be when you grow up?”
Then I said . . .

"When I grow up I want to be you, Dr. DaBison.
You have the best toys in the universe!"